Berlin Wall   1970

Siena, Italy 1996

Marseille 1999

Monastery at Singhik, Tibetan border. 1974

For Colin McNaughton—
and dreamers everywhere

Copyright © 2002 by Michael Foreman
All rights reserved
First published in Great Britain by Andersen Press, 2002
Color separations by Photolitho AG
Printed and bound in Italy by Grafiche AZ
First American edition, 2003
1 3 5 7 9 10 8 6 4 2

Library of Congress Cataloging-in-Publication Data
Foreman, Michael, 1938–
    Wonder goal! / Michael Foreman.
        p. cm.
    Summary: A boy describes what it feels like to score a goal that
makes his soccer teammates stop teasing him.
    ISBN 0-374-38500-9
    [1. Soccer—Fiction.] I. Title.

PZ7.F7583 Wo 2003
[Fic]—dc21
                                                            2002069725

Michael Foreman

WONDER GOAL!

Farrar, Straus and Giroux
New York

It was a cold Sunday.
The boy hadn't noticed his
teammates tie his laces together
on the way to the game. So
when he tripped and fell out of
the contractor's van that was
their team bus, it just made
him even more determined to
show them.

They were good guys really,
but he was new to the team
and they always teased the
new boy.

And when they ran out to start
the game, he knew they all
dreamed the same dream,
the same impossible dream
of one day becoming world-class
soccer stars.

In the second half, he got his chance to show them.

It was perfect. Head over the ball, balance, power, timing. All the things his dad had told him.

As soon as he kicked it,
he knew it was going to be
a goal. It was a screamer.
No goalie in the world
could save that shot.

Maybe *now* his teammates
would stop teasing him.

Then, in his mind,
everything seemed to stop,
frozen in time.

The goalie seemed to hang
in the air, and the ball hovered
just beyond his fingertips.

It was like a photograph . . .

. . . like all those photographs
that crowded the walls
of his tiny bedroom,
where he dreamed every night
of scoring a wonder goal and
winning the World Cup.

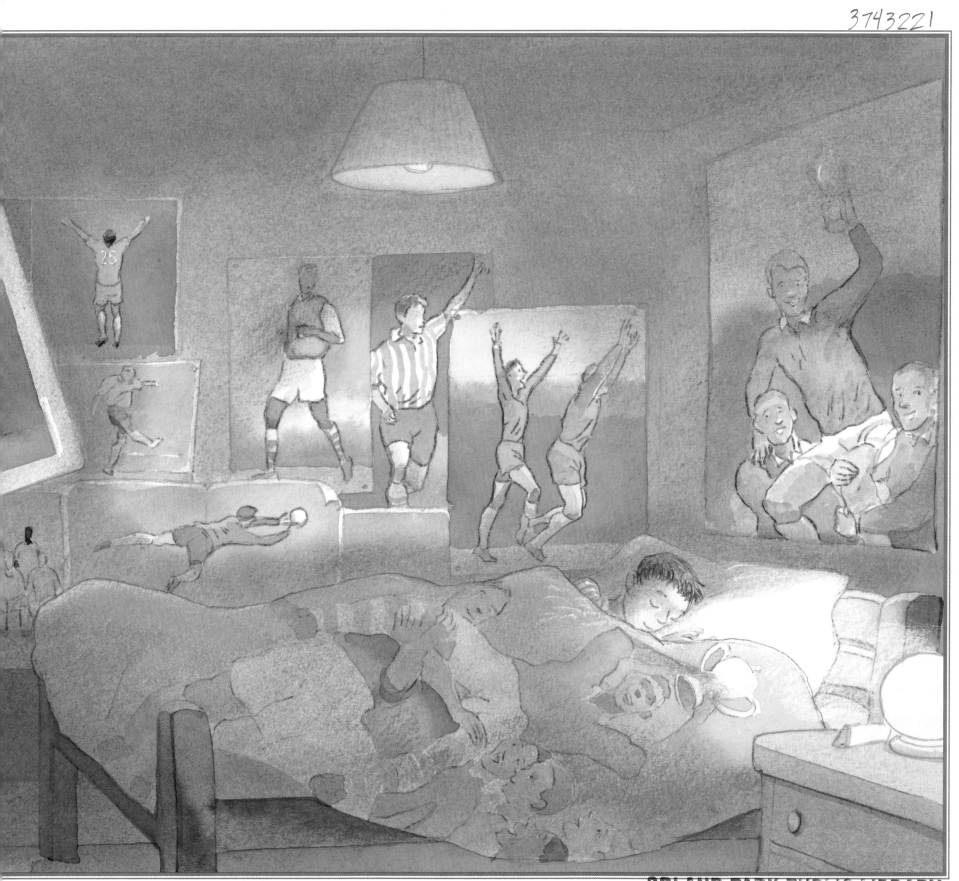

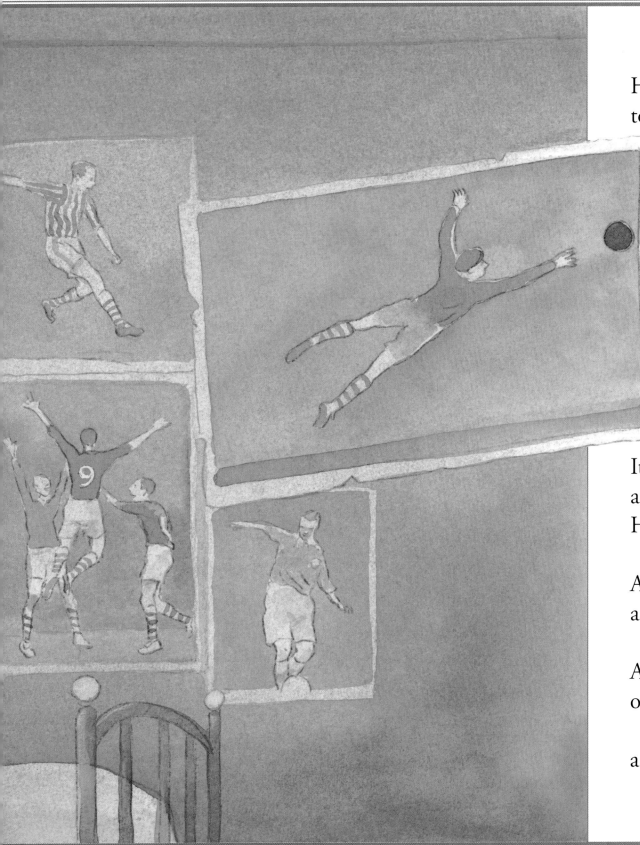

He knew his dad used
to have the same dream
   when he was a boy,
   and that he, too, had slept
   in a room wall to wall
   with heroes.

   His dad usually came to all
   the games, but this weekend
   he had to work overtime.

   His dad was not going to
   see the wonder goal.
It wouldn't be in the papers
and it wouldn't be on the telly.
His dad was going to miss it.

All this flashed through his mind
as the ball flew toward the goal.

And then time clicked into gear
once more and moved on . . .

and on . . .

The goalie hit the ground . . .

. . . and the ball smacked
into the back of the net.

The vast crowd erupted. He had hit another wonder goal!

Just like the goal he had scored all those years before on that freezing boyhood Sunday.

Maybe now, after such a goal, his teammates would stop teasing him.

They were good guys really, but he was the newest member of the squad and they always teased the new guy.

And anyway, he knew they had always shared the same dream of winning the World Cup . . .

They hadn't won it yet, but he *had* just scored the first goal of the Final . . . And this time it would be in all the papers, and on the news.

And this time—*this* time, his dad was there to see it.

Soccer in the Straits of Malacca

...ball in the City of the Dead   Cairo